Jacob Grant

FEIWEL AND FRIENDS
NEW YORK

A FEIWEL AND FRIENDS BOOK
An Imprint of Macmillan

Printed in China by RR Donnelley Asia Printing Solutions Ltd., Dongguan City,
Guangdong Province. For information, address Feiwel and Friends,
175 Fifth Avenue, New York, N.Y. 10010.

Our books may be purchased in bulk for promotional, educational, or business use.
Please contact your local bookseller or the Macmillan Corporate and Premium
Sales Department at (800) 221-7945 ext. 5442 or by e-mail
at MacmillanSpecialMarkets@macmillan.com.

Library of Congress Cataloging-in-Publication Data Available

ISBN: 978-1-250-05150-9

Book design by Jacob Grant and Anna Booth

The art was drawn with charcoal and crayon and colored digitally.
Feiwel and Friends logo designed by Filomena Tuosto

First Edition: 2016

1   3   5   7   9   10   8   6   4   2

mackids.com

For Brother,
my constant friend and occasional headache.

Cat and Girl had always been good friends.

One day, Girl brought home
a colorful new guest.

His name was Yarn.

Cat was fascinated by Yarn.

He'd never had a friend so
bright and rolly.

The two of them were inseparable.

But Girl also wanted
to play with Yarn.

Cat waited and waited.

He wasn't sure what
Girl was up to,
but he didn't like it.

When Yarn returned,
he wasn't his usual
bouncy self.

Cat's friend had changed.

Cat did not like this new Yarn one bit.

He was itchy and stuffy and no fun at all.

Cat was so mad, he hardly
noticed the cold snow.

He had to get away from
this new Yarn.

Soon, Cat realized just how
cold it was.

Warming up to something new
takes time.

Yarn may have changed,
but they would always
be friends.

Then one day, Girl
brought home a group
of colorful guests.